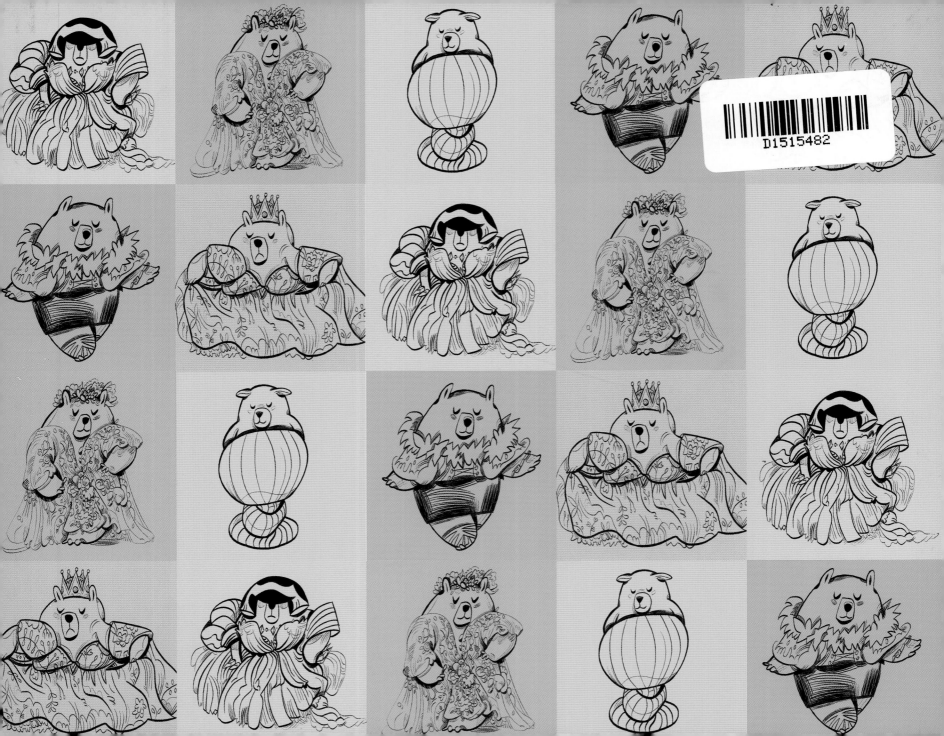

Prince Sacha's Fierce, Fabulous, Fancy Day

Story and Pictures by Jon Lau

Orchard Books / New York
An Imprint of Scholastic Inc.

For Sam, Timmy, Dad, Aimee, Junyi, Nikko, Lynn, Szu, Mon-Lai, Steven, Elle, Eric, Ben, Lorrie, Gayle, Darshana, Yuyu, Matthew, House of 3-2-1, and Kait.

Library of Congress Cataloging-in-Publication Data available
ISBN 978-1-338-32474-7
10 9 8 7 6 5 4 3 2 1   23 24 25 26 27

Printed in China   38
First edition, August 2023

Book design by Charles Kreloff
The text and display type were set in Macondo.
The artwork was created as individual characters, textures, objects, and backgrounds, painted on art paper with poster paints. Each piece was then scanned, and the digital files were collaged together using Adobe Photoshop.

Prince Sacha . . .

. . . was the most fabulous bear in all the land.

He lived in the finest palace.
He ate the fanciest food.

And he wore the fiercest clothes.

Prince Sacha's gift for fashion was so revered that he simply had to create an event to showcase his sparkling style: the annual Parade of Princely Prancing!

Animals from all over the kingdom would come in their very best outfits for the occasion, and they were eager to have their prince prance down the runway in his most fabulous gown yet.

There was just one problem this year . . .

This had never happened before. He was beyond distraught. "Am I supposed to walk down that runway naked?" he asked no one in particular. So Prince Sacha decided to hold an emergency contest.

GRAND PRIZE
I (me, Sacha) will wear your outfit. We will make history. And you get a lifetime supply of boba.
xo, Prince Sacha.

He invited every fashion designer in the
kingdom to come up with the most fabulous
outfits, and he'd select the best one.

Designers came from far and wide to
compete for the double honor of dressing *the*
Prince Sacha and receiving a lifetime supply of
his legendary boba milk tea.

One by one, they presented their works for
Prince Sacha to try on.

But nothing would do.

Squeak

Squeak

"A prince does not squeak!"

"Why is this wig so sticky?"

"Not enough glitter!"

"I can't wear my heels with this!"

There was only one designer left: the confident and sly rabbit named Panini.

"Look here, Your Fabulousness!" said Panini. "This gown is woven from the fanciest fabric a bear can wear."

Prince Sacha perked up but didn't see anything. "WHERE?"

"Why, it's right here." Panini pointed. "This fabric is so fancy, so fine, that only the most fabulous animals can see it."

Prince Sacha squinted harder.
He looked closer, but . . .

. . . he couldn't see a thing.

If this was the finest fabric, why couldn't Prince Sacha, the fanciest bear, see it? He sank into his throne, lost in thought.

Members of Sacha's royal court couldn't see the gown either. Panini whispered loud enough for all to hear, "I'm shocked he can't see it! Maybe our prince has lost his fabulousness!"

Lost?! Impossible! thought Prince Sacha. He needed to prove his fabulousness did not, in fact, need finding.

"I see it now!" he declared. "When I wear this at the parade, this will go down in history as my most fabulous look of all time."

Prince Sacha kicked up his heels and cheered, "Panini, you win! You get a lifetime supply of my famous boba milk tea!"

There was still much prancing to practice, but that night Prince Sacha treated himself to some bear-time. There was nothing more relaxing and cleansing than a hot onion bath.

Meanwhile, Panini and his helpers pretend-worked all day and all night to complete Prince Sacha's best look in time for the parade.

At last, the big day was here!

All the animals in the kingdom arrived in their most fabulous outfits and gathered in Prince Sacha's court for his one-bear spectacle.

Panini and his staff pretended to help Prince Sacha into his gown.

As he slipped on an oddly plain pair of heels, he winked and squealed, "A perfect fit!"

Prince Sacha marched down the parade runway in a fiery swish. The crowd went quiet. Prince Sacha blew kisses, posed, and waved. No one said a word.

Finally, a bird cheeped, "The Prince is bare!"
Everyone gasped.

Prince Sacha whirled around impatiently
and asked, "Do you mean to say you don't see me rocking
the most fabulous look of all time?"

"But, Your Beariness," said the giraffe, "why did you
take it off, then?"

Prince Sacha struck a pose as he answered, "That's just it! I can never take off my fabulousness. Gown or no gown, I am the most fabulous bear, and you are each your most fabulous selves."

He spun on his heel and pranced back to his palace. His subjects were speechless.

The crowd slowly, then all at once, erupted into loud cheers and applause.

The baboon cried, "It's true — I'm still wearing my fabulousness!"

"Me too!" the red panda yipped.

"If Prince Sacha can be fabulous no matter what, so can we!" the meerkats chattered.

Prince Sacha slipped into some more festive heels as he led the parade and partied with his friends.

From then on, all the animals returned every year to Prince Sacha's court to prance together in the parade, wearing nothing but their fabulousness.

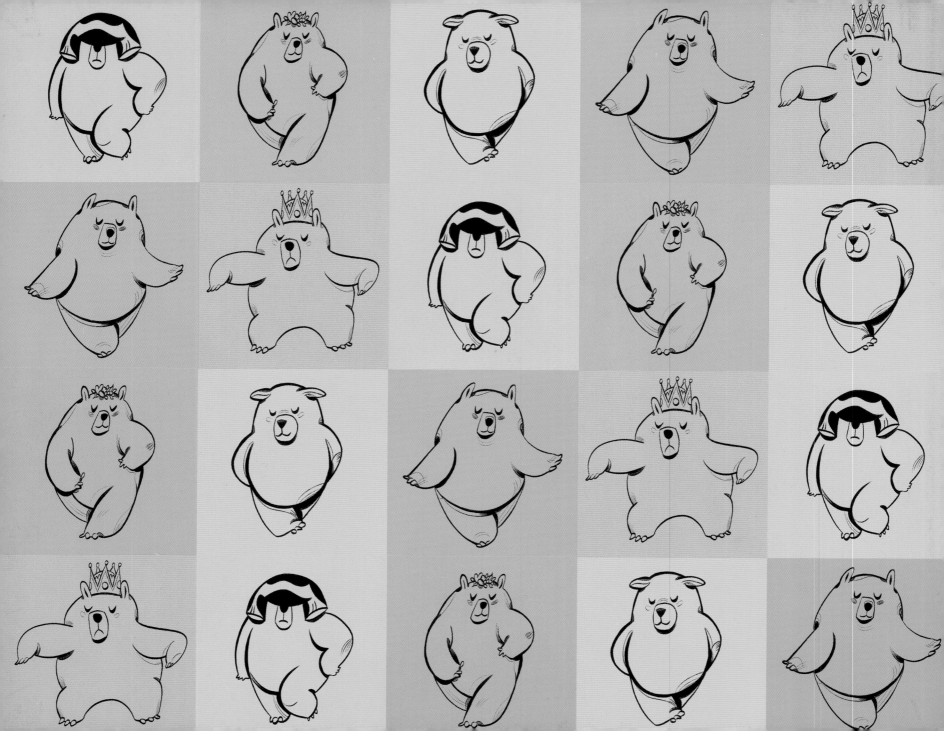